I0663174

Number 13

*A Haunting Tale of Vanishing Rooms
and Supernatural Secrets*

A Modern Translation

Adapted for the Contemporary Reader

M.R. James

Translated by Tim Zengerink

Table of Contents

Preface - Message to the Reader

What If You Could Help Rebuild the Greatest Library in Human History?

Thousands of years ago, the Library of Alexandria stood as the crown jewel of human achievement — a sanctuary where the collected wisdom of every known civilization was gathered, preserved, and shared freely.

And then, it was lost.

Through fire, conquest, and the slow erosion of time, humanity lost not just books — but ideas, dreams, discoveries, and stories that could have changed the world forever.

Today, the Library of Alexandria lives again — and you are invited to be a part of its restoration.

Our mission is simple yet profound:

To rebuild the greatest library the world has ever known, and to translate all timeless works into every language and dialect, so that no seeker of knowledge is ever left behind again.

By joining our movement to rebuild the modern Library of Alexandria, you become part of an unprecedented mission:

- **Unlimited Access to the Greatest Audiobooks & eBooks Ever Written:**

  Instantly explore thousands of legendary works—Plato, Shakespeare, Jane Austen, Leo Tolstoy, and countless more. All instantly available to read or listen, placing a complete literary universe at your fingertips.

- **Beautiful Paperback & Deluxe Editions at Printing Cost**

  Own any title as an elegant paperback, deluxe hardcover, or stunning collectible boxset—offered to you at true printing cost, delivered straight to your door. Build your personal Library of Alexandria, crafted for beauty, built for durability, and worthy of proud display.

- **Fresh Translations for Modern Readers—in Every Language & Dialect**

  Enjoy timeless masterpieces reimagined in clear, contemporary language—no more outdated phrases or obscure references. Alongside the original versions, we're tirelessly translating these classics into every language and dialect imaginable, ensuring accessibility and understanding across cultures and generations.

- **Join a Global Renaissance of Literature & Knowledge**

  You directly support expanding our library, publishing deluxe editions at true cost, translating works into all global languages, and bringing humanity's greatest stories to people everywhere. By joining today, you're not just preserving a legacy of masterpieces; you set in motion a powerful wave of literary accessibility.

Become a Torchbearer of Knowledge.

Join us for free now at **LibraryofAlexandria.com**

Together, we will ensure that the light of human wisdom never fades again.

With gratitude and a shared love of knowledge,

The Modern Library of Alexandria Team

Visit:

www.libraryofalexandria.com

Or scan the code below:

Introduction

The Disappearing Room and
the Architecture of Dread

M.R. James's Number 13, first published in 1904 in his debut collection Ghost Stories of an Antiquary, is a perfectly executed supernatural mystery that plays with space, logic, and perception to craft one of the most haunting and surreal stories in James's corpus. While many of his tales revolve around cursed objects, buried manuscripts, or vengeful ghosts, Number 13 explores a different horror: the unreliability of physical reality itself. What if the world we inhabit—the very structure of our surroundings—can be warped by supernatural forces? What if space itself becomes unstable?

Set in an inn in Viborg, Denmark, the story follows Mr. Anderson, a rational, scholarly Englishman who arrives to conduct historical research on the Reformation. While staying at the inn, he begins to notice peculiarities: the number of rooms does not add up, strange noises come from the adjoining wall, and shadows seem to move where they should not. Most unsettlingly, a room that should not exist—Room 13—

seems to appear and vanish at will. From within it come sounds of movement, muttered voices, and an eerie vibration of malevolent intent.

James draws deeply on European folklore and historical religious conflict in this tale, embedding within it the dark legacies of heresy, inquisitions, and occult knowledge. Yet the true brilliance of Number 13 lies in how it maintains ambiguity: Is the room a physical anomaly, a hallucination, or an intersection with another plane of existence? James never offers a concrete answer, preferring instead to let the reader—and his protagonist—stand at the edge of understanding, watching as the impossible unfolds in quiet horror.

This introduction will examine Number 13 in depth, exploring how James manipulates architecture and perception to build dread. We will consider the story's use of spatial uncertainty, its historical subtext, and its elegant narrative structure. Finally, we will explore its broader influence on later horror literature and film, particularly in the "haunted space" subgenre. As we shall see, Number 13 is more than a ghost story—it is a meditation on instability, intrusion, and the silent forces that lurk just outside the boundaries of what we deem real.

The Unreliable Room:
Space, Sanity, and Supernatural Architecture

At the heart of Number 13 lies an architectural anomaly—a room that both exists and doesn't. The protagonist, Mr. Anderson, notices early on that the inn's room numbers seem off. Though he is assigned Room 12, there should logically be a Room 13 between his and Room 14. Yet the hotel's owner assures him that no such room exists—of course not, given the superstition against that number. And indeed, during the day, only Rooms 12 and 14 are visible. But at night, strange things occur.

The furniture in Anderson's room shifts on its own. His belongings go missing and reappear. More disturbingly, he hears sounds from the room next door—scraping, chanting, footsteps—though no one is supposed to be there. At one point, the physical dimensions of his room change, as if the wall has shifted to make space for another room. The architecture bends itself. A door appears that should not exist. Room 13, it seems, comes into being only under certain conditions—at night, in shadow, perhaps in response to presence or attention.

This manipulation of space is both literal and psychological. As Anderson tries to investigate, the stability of his surroundings—and of his own perceptions—comes under question. James plays masterfully with ambiguity: is Anderson hallucinating? Is he under the influence of old superstitions? Or is something genuinely, impossibly, shifting in the fabric of the inn?

James is not interested in jump scares or grotesque revelations. Instead, he builds unease through contradiction: the rational mind confronts the irrational structure. The room, in this case, is not a container for ghosts. It is the ghost. Its very presence violates the rules of space and logic. And this, perhaps, is what makes Number 13 so frightening—not the idea of a haunting, but the idea that physical reality can warp, that buildings can lie, and that the familiar can suddenly mutate into the uncanny.

In the end, Room 13 vanishes. A team of investigators—including Anderson—attempts to examine the space, and the horror culminates in an episode of violent activity: a grotesque figure is glimpsed through the distorted doorway, furniture is hurled, and the room implodes into non-existence. What was once there is gone, leaving only unanswered questions and an absence that seems too purposeful.

Faith, Heresy, and the Ghosts of History

Though the supernatural elements of Number 13 are central, James subtly embeds them in a rich historical framework. Anderson is in Viborg to research documents related to the Reformation—a time of upheaval, persecution, and theological warfare. The town, with its ancient cathedral and long memory, stands as a symbol of layered time: a place where the past is never fully gone.

James, a medievalist and devout Anglican, often drew on ecclesiastical history for his stories, and in Number 13, the implication is that the room's haunting may stem from old sins committed during the Reformation. One theory suggested in the text is that Room 13 occasionally becomes the domain of a heretical figure—perhaps a sorcerer, perhaps a persecutor—whose presence still infects the space. The murmuring voices heard through the wall, the chanting, and the ancient, claw-like figure glimpsed in the climax all point toward something occult, connected to forbidden knowledge and religious blasphemy.

But James never provides a definitive origin. The story resists explanation, and in doing so, gains potency. Rather than tying the haunting to a specific crime or ghost, he suggests that certain places absorb the trauma of history—that violence, injustice, and dark faiths can leave scars in space. The supernatural becomes not a visitation, but a resurgence—a past that rewrites the present.

This view of haunting is sophisticated. It moves beyond the idea of restless spirits and into the realm of temporal contamination. Room 13 is not simply cursed. It is historically ruptured. It is a fault line through which something old leaks—something that predates understanding, and perhaps resists it.

James's religious background enriches this theme. His ghosts often emerge when the sacred is profaned, when history is desecrated, or when arrogance replaces humility. In Number 13, the very act of seeking knowledge (Anderson's research) seems to trigger a breach in reality. As in Casting the Runes and The Mezzotint, curiosity is not an innocent trait. It is dangerous. And what it uncovers is not wisdom—but horror.

Literary Lineage and Influence: Haunted Spaces in Modern Horror

Though it remains one of James's shorter and more contained stories, Number 13 has had an outsized influence on the development of horror fiction—

especially in the subgenre of haunted or anomalous spaces. Its central idea—that a room can exist and not exist, and that space itself can become haunted—has been echoed in countless later works, from Stephen King's 1408 to the psychological architecture of films like The Shining and Session 9. Even cosmic horror, as developed by Lovecraft and others, owes a debt to James's suggestion that reality can be thin, penetrable, and mutable.

The fear in Number 13 is not of death, but of uncertainty. It is the fear that the world does not function as we believe—that the logical frameworks of daily life (room numbers, walls, dimensions) can break down under pressure. This kind of horror is enduring because it undermines the very foundations of safety. A ghost can be exorcised. A monster can be fought. But a room that should not exist—a room that appears and disappears without warning—offers no such resolution. It is horror made spatial, mathematical, and insoluble.

James's restraint is also essential to the story's success. He never shows us too much. The grotesque figure glimpsed in Room 13 is seen only in fragments. The events that caused the haunting are never fully revealed. The room disappears without a trace. This ambiguity is not a weakness—it is the engine of the story's longevity. The reader, like Anderson, is left with unease, not closure.

In this way, Number 13 stands as a brilliant distillation of James's aesthetic: a ghost story that haunts not with spectacle, but with implication. It invites re-reading, analysis, and, most of all, contemplation. What makes a room real? What defines a boundary? And if our world is built on assumptions about structure, what happens when those assumptions prove false?

The answer, as James would have it, is simple and chilling.

You may find yourself in a room that no one else can see.

You may not remember walking into it.

And once you're inside, the door might not open again.

Number 13

Viborg is one of the most important towns in Jutland. It's the center of a bishopric and has a beautiful—though mostly new—cathedral, a lovely garden, a scenic lake, and lots of storks. Close by is Hald, said to be one of Denmark's prettiest spots, and also Finderup, where Marsk Stig killed King Erik Glipping on St. Cecilia's Day in 1286. When the king's tomb was opened in the 1600s, they found fifty-six square-headed mace blows on his skull. But I'm not writing a travel guide.

Viborg has some great hotels—Preisler's and the Phoenix are both excellent. But my cousin, whose story I'm about to tell, stayed at the Golden Lion the first time he visited. He never returned, and these pages might explain why.

The Golden Lion is one of the few buildings in Viborg that survived the huge fire of 1726, which destroyed most of the old city, including the cathedral and many other historic buildings. The front of the hotel is made of red brick, with steps along the gables and a Bible verse over the door. The courtyard, where the carriage drops guests off, has black-and-white wood and plaster walls in a checkered pattern.

When my cousin, Mr. Anderson, arrived, the sun was low in the sky, casting warm light on the building's grand front. He loved the old look of the place and expected a fun and comfortable stay in such a classic Danish inn.

Mr. Anderson wasn't in Viborg for regular business. He was doing research on the history of the Catholic Church in Denmark and had learned that the Viborg State Archives had some papers saved from the fire that related to the final days of Catholicism in the country. He planned to spend two or three weeks there copying documents. He hoped the Golden Lion could provide him with a large enough room to use both as a bedroom and a study.

He explained this to the innkeeper, who, after thinking a bit, suggested that Mr. Anderson take a look at a few rooms himself and pick the one he liked best. That sounded fair.

The top floor was ruled out because it was too tiring to climb after a long day of work. The second floor didn't have a room with the right size. But on the first floor, there were a few rooms that looked like they'd work well.

The innkeeper recommended Room 17, but Mr. Anderson didn't like that its windows faced a blank wall, making it very dark in the afternoons. Rooms 12 and 14 looked out over the street, and he preferred the natural light and view—even if it meant more noise. In the end, he picked Room 12.

It had three windows on one wall, was fairly tall, and longer than average. There was no fireplace, but it had a nicely detailed cast-iron stove with an image of Abraham about to sacrifice Isaac and a Bible verse above it: "1st Book of Moses, Chapter 22." Nothing else in the room really stood out, except for an old colored print of the town from around 1820.

It was almost dinner time, but before the bell rang, Mr. Anderson washed up and went downstairs. He still had a few minutes, so he checked out the guest list. Like most Danish hotels, names were written on a big blackboard with each guest listed under their room number. The list was pretty dull: a lawyer, a German traveler, and some salesmen from Copenhagen.

The only odd thing was that there was no Room 13, but Anderson had seen that before in Danish hotels. He started wondering if the number 13 was avoided so often that it made Room 13 impossible to rent, and he planned to ask the innkeeper about it.

He didn't say much about dinner, and his evening was mostly spent unpacking his clothes, books, and research papers. Around eleven, he decided it was time to sleep—but like many people today, he found it hard to fall asleep without reading a bit first. Then he remembered: the book he'd been reading on the train—the only one he really wanted to finish—was still in the pocket of his coat, which he'd hung on a peg outside the dining room.

Anderson quickly ran down to grab his book and, since the hallways were well-lit, he had no trouble finding his way back to what he thought was his room. But when he turned the handle, the door wouldn't open. He could hear someone quickly moving inside. He had tried the wrong room. Was his room on the right or left? He looked at the number: it was 13. His room must be to the left—and it was. He went inside and, after a few minutes in bed, reading the usual few pages from his book, he turned out the light and got ready to sleep.

Then it hit him—there hadn't been a Room 13 listed on the hotel's blackboard earlier, but here it clearly was. He felt a little bad he hadn't picked that room himself. Maybe it would've helped the innkeeper rent it more easily if he could say that a respectable Englishman had stayed there and liked it. Still, it was probably just used by staff or wasn't as nice as his room anyway.

As he looked around in the dim glow from the

streetlamp, he noticed something odd. Usually rooms look bigger in low light, but this one seemed smaller—and maybe even taller. He shrugged it off, thinking sleep was more important than strange thoughts, and soon fell asleep.

The next day, Anderson started his work at the Viborg State Archives. As expected in Denmark, he was welcomed warmly, and they gave him easy access to everything he needed. He found way more papers than he expected—especially a lot of old letters and notes about Bishop Jörgen Friis, the last Catholic bishop in the area. These letters were full of interesting and sometimes juicy details about the people of that time.

One letter talked a lot about a house owned by the bishop but not lived in by him. The person renting it had a bad reputation. The locals believed he practiced dark magic and had even sold his soul to the devil. People said it was just more proof of the corruption in the Catholic Church. They called the tenant a monster and accused the bishop of protecting him. But the bishop defended himself, saying he hated anything to do with magic or the devil and dared his critics to take the case to court. He claimed he'd be happy to see this man, a certain Nicolas Francken, punished—if the charges were true.

Anderson didn't get to read much of the next letter by Protestant leader Rasmus Nielsen before the archive closed for the day. But he could tell the letter said people didn't have to follow Catholic bishops anymore and that the bishop's court wasn't the right place to judge something so serious.

As Anderson walked out, the old archivist, Herr Scavenius, walked with him. They talked about the old letters. Though Herr Scavenius knew a lot about the archives in general, he wasn't an expert on that time in history. He was very interested in Anderson's discoveries and said he looked forward to seeing the finished work once it was published.

They talked about Bishop Friis's mysterious house. Herr Scavenius had tried to figure out where it once stood, but said it was tough to tell. Part of an old map from 1560 that might have shown it was missing from the archive. Still, he hoped to figure it out one day.

After taking a walk—Anderson couldn't recall where exactly—he returned to the Golden Lion, ate supper, played a bit of solitaire, and went to bed.

As he headed to his room, he remembered he hadn't asked the landlord about Room 13 and figured he should at least check if it actually existed before saying anything.

It was easy to find. The door was clearly labeled 13, and something was going on inside. He heard footsteps—and maybe a voice—coming from the room. As he stood there checking the number, the footsteps stopped, and he heard a strange, fast breathing, like someone excited or angry. A bit startled, he quickly went to his room.

Once again, he was surprised by how much smaller it felt now. It was a little disappointing, but not a big deal—if it really bothered him, he could ask for another room. Right now, though, he needed something from his suitcase, which the porter had placed on a small stand at the far end of the room.

But the suitcase was gone.

He figured the cleaning staff must have moved it and checked the wardrobe—but it wasn't there either. That was annoying. He didn't think it had been stolen. Denmark wasn't a place where that happened often. Still, someone had clearly messed up, and he decided he'd have to speak to the maid about it later.

Whatever he needed could wait until morning. He didn't want to bother the staff now.

He walked to the window on the right side of the room and looked out onto the quiet street. There was a tall building across from him, mostly blank wall. The night was dark, the street empty, and there was nothing much to see.

The light from the room was behind Anderson, so he could clearly see his own shadow on the wall across the street. He also saw the shadow of the man staying in Room 11 on the left. That man walked back and forth in his shirtsleeves, brushed his hair, and later appeared in a nightgown.

Then Anderson noticed the shadow of whoever was in Room 13 on the right. That one was more interesting. Like Anderson, the person was leaning on the windowsill, looking out into the street. He seemed tall and thin—or maybe it was a woman? Whoever it was had a cloth or scarf covering their head, like they were about to go to bed. Anderson thought they must've had a red lamp in the room, and it flickered a lot, because a dull red light moved up and down on the opposite wall. He leaned out a little, hoping to get a better look, but he couldn't see much except for a piece of white fabric resting on the windowsill.

Then he heard footsteps far off in the street. The sound seemed to startle the person in Room 13, because they quickly pulled away from the window and the red light went out. Anderson, who had been smoking a cigarette, left the stub on the windowsill and went to bed.

The next morning, the maid came in with hot water and other things. Anderson sat up and, thinking carefully about the Danish words, said:

"Please don't move my suitcase. Where is it?"

As often happens, the maid just laughed and left without answering clearly.

Anderson, feeling annoyed, sat up in bed and was about to call her back—but then he froze. The suitcase was right there on the little stand, exactly where the porter had placed it when Anderson first arrived. It was a shock. He'd been so sure it was missing the night before. How had he not seen it? He had no answer—but there it was.

Daylight also revealed more about the room. With all three windows lit, Anderson could see the room's true size, and it turned out to be just as good as he had hoped when choosing it. Once he was almost dressed, he walked over to the middle window to check the weather—and got another surprise. He would've sworn that he'd been smoking at the right-hand window before bed. But there was his cigarette stub sitting on the sill of the middle window.

Later, as he headed down to breakfast—running a

bit late—he noticed the boots outside Room 13. They were clearly men's boots. So, Room 13's occupant was a man, not a woman. Then he glanced at the door. It said 14. Strange. Had he just passed Room 13 without seeing it? That didn't seem right. To be sure, he turned back and checked.

The room next to 14 was his own—Room 12. There was no Room 13 at all.

After thinking hard about everything he'd eaten and drunk in the past day, Anderson gave up trying to explain it. If he was starting to see or imagine things, he'd find out soon enough. But if not—if this was something real—then it was clearly something unusual and worth paying attention to.

That day, he continued studying the bishop's old letters, the ones he'd been reading before. He was disappointed to find there were no more letters about Magister Nicolas Francken. The only other one was from Bishop Jörgen Friis to Rasmus Nielsen. The bishop wrote:

"Even though we don't agree with your opinion about our church court, and we're ready to defend it if needed, it no longer matters—because our dear Magister Nicolas Francken, the one you've accused of serious and false crimes, has suddenly died. So the case is over for now. But since you also claimed that Saint John, in his Book of Revelation, described the Holy Roman Church as the Scarlet Woman, we must inform you..." and the letter went on from there.

Anderson couldn't find any follow-up to this letter or any clue about how Francken had died. Since there were only two days between the last letter—where Francken was still alive—and this one, it must have been a sudden and unexpected death.

That afternoon, Anderson took a short trip to Hald and had tea at Baekkelund. Even though he was feeling a little on edge, he didn't notice anything wrong with his eyesight or thinking that might explain the strange events that morning.

At supper, he found himself sitting next to the hotel owner.

After some small talk, Anderson asked, "Why is it that most hotels in Denmark skip Room 13? I see you don't have one here either."

The landlord chuckled.

"It's funny you noticed that! I've thought about it a few times myself. A smart man, I think, shouldn't care about silly superstitions. When I was in school here in Viborg, our old teacher was really strict about that stuff.

He was a tough, no-nonsense guy. I remember us boys one snowy day—"

He drifted into a story.

"So you don't think there's anything wrong with having a Room 13?" Anderson asked when the story ended.

"Well," the landlord said, "my dad ran a hotel too. First in Aarhuus, then here in Viborg—this was his hometown. He owned the Phœnix until he died in 1876. Then I opened my own place in Silkeborg, and just last year, I moved into this house."

He explained more about how he got started here, then added:

"When I moved in, there was no Room 13—and I didn't add one either. You see, most of our guests are business travelers. Try putting one of them in Room 13? They'd rather sleep outside! Doesn't matter to me—I'd sleep in any room. But they all swear it brings bad luck. They've got loads of stories—men who stayed in Room 13 and never recovered, lost their best clients, or worse."

The landlord searched for the right words to explain it better, then simply shrugged.

"Then what do you use Room 13 for?" Anderson asked, feeling strangely nervous about something that seemed like such a small question.

"Room 13?" the landlord said. "Didn't I already tell you? There's no Room 13 in this hotel. I thought you would've noticed that. If there were, it would be right next to your room."

"Well, yes," Anderson replied. "It's just... last night, I thought I saw a door with a number 13 on it in the hallway. And I'm pretty sure I saw it the night before, too."

As expected, Herr Kristensen laughed and brushed it off like it was nonsense. He firmly repeated that there never had been a Room 13 in the hotel, not before he arrived and not now.

Anderson felt a little better hearing that, but he still couldn't shake his confusion. He decided the only way to know for sure if he'd imagined it was to invite the landlord to his room later that night for a cigar. He could use his photos of English towns as a reason.

The landlord was pleased by the offer and happily agreed to come at ten o'clock. Before that, Anderson had some letters to write, so he went back to his room. He felt a little embarrassed to admit it even to himself, but the whole thing was starting to make him genuinely uneasy. He was so unsettled that he took a longer path to avoid walking past where Room 13 should have been.

Once inside his room, he quickly looked around, suspicious. But everything was normal—except that strange feeling again, like the room was smaller than before. He made sure his suitcase was still there, tucked safely under the bed where he had put it himself. He tried to put the strange thoughts out of his mind and focused on his writing.

Everything in the hallway was quiet. Every now and then, someone opened a door and tossed out a pair of boots, or a salesman strolled by humming. Outside, carts clattered loudly over the uneven cobblestones, and the occasional footsteps echoed on the sidewalk.

After finishing his letters, Anderson ordered a whisky and soda. He went to the window to look out at the empty wall across from his room and the shadows cast upon it.

If he remembered correctly, Room 14 was being used by a lawyer—a quiet man who barely spoke during meals and usually read papers by his plate. But from what Anderson could see in the window's reflection, the man must act differently when alone. Why else would he be dancing?

The shadow clearly showed a thin figure moving back and forth across the window. Arms waved. One skinny leg kicked high in the air. He looked barefoot.

The floor must have been built well because there wasn't a sound.

Seeing Sagförer Herr Anders Jensen, the serious lawyer, dancing around his room at ten o'clock at night seemed almost poetic. Anderson found it oddly amusing, and like the heroine Emily in The Mysteries of Udolpho, his mind began forming a few silly lines of verse.

When I come back to my hotel
Around ten each night,
The waiters think I'm not quite well—
But I just smile, that's all right.
I shut my door and toss out my boots,
Then dance across the floor.
And even if my neighbors shout,
I'll only dance some more.
You see, I know the rules quite well,
So let them talk or moan—
No matter what they say or yell,
I'll dance all on my own.

If the landlord hadn't knocked just then, Anderson might have finished a whole poem. When Herr Kristensen stepped into the room, he looked surprised, clearly noticing the same odd feeling that had struck Anderson, though he said nothing. The photos

Anderson had brought caught the landlord's attention and sparked long stories about his own life.

They might not have gotten around to talking about Room 13 if the lawyer next door hadn't suddenly started singing—and not in any normal way. The sound was high-pitched and thin, like a voice that hadn't been used in a long time. It climbed to a strange, almost screeching note and dropped again with a wailing moan, like wind howling through a chimney or an organ running out of air. It was awful to hear. Anderson was grateful not to be alone—if he had been, he might have run straight into a neighbor's room just to escape it.

The landlord looked stunned.

"I don't get it," he said, wiping sweat from his face. "It's awful. I heard something like it once before, but I thought it was just a cat."

"Do you think he's gone mad?" Anderson asked.

"He must have," the landlord replied. "It's a shame—he's a good customer and, I hear, does well in business. He has a young family, too."

Right then, someone knocked hard at the door and barged in without waiting. It was the lawyer—disheveled and clearly upset.

"Excuse me," he said angrily, "but could you please

stop that—"

He cut himself off when he saw they weren't the ones making the noise. Just then, the strange singing rose again, louder and more haunting than before.

"What on earth is going on?" the lawyer shouted. "Where is it coming from? Who's doing it? Am I losing my mind?"

"It must be coming from your room," Anderson said. "Maybe there's a cat stuck in the chimney?"

He knew it was a weak guess, but it was better than standing there listening to that dreadful voice, while watching the landlord tremble and grip his chair, his face pale with fear.

"No way," said the lawyer. "There is no chimney. I came here because I was sure the noise was coming from this room. It's right next to mine."

"Is there a door between our rooms?" Anderson asked quickly.

"No," said the lawyer, clearly irritated. "At least, not this morning."

"Ah," said Anderson. "And now?"

"I'm… not sure," said the lawyer, hesitating.

Just then, the voice stopped. A moment later, they

heard the same person laugh quietly, as if to themselves. It was a soft, creepy sound, and all three men shivered.

Then there was silence.

"Well?" said the lawyer. "What do you say to this, Herr Kristensen? What's going on?"

"Heavens, how should I know?" said the landlord. "I'm just as confused as you are. I hope I never hear anything like that again."

"Same here," the lawyer muttered. He added something softly under his breath. Anderson thought it might have been the words, 'Let every spirit praise the Lord'—but he couldn't be sure.

"But we have to do something," said Anderson. "The three of us should go check the next room."

"But that's Herr Jensen's room," the landlord protested. "There's no point—he just came from there."

"I'm not so sure," said Jensen. "I think this man is right. We should go look."

The only weapons they could find were a stick and an umbrella. Nervously, they stepped into the hallway. Everything was completely quiet, but there was a light coming from under the next door. Anderson and Jensen walked over. Jensen grabbed the doorknob and gave it a strong push. Nothing happened. The door wouldn't budge.

"Herr Kristensen," Jensen said, "can you go get the strongest worker you have? We need help."

The landlord quickly nodded and left, clearly relieved to get away. Anderson and Jensen stayed in the hallway, staring at the door.

"It really is Number 13," said Anderson.

"Yes. There's your door, and there's mine," said Jensen.

"My room has three windows during the day," said Anderson, trying not to laugh nervously.

"So does mine!" said Jensen, turning to face him. His back was now to the door. At that moment, the door behind him suddenly opened, and a hand reached out, grabbing at his shoulder. The arm wore ragged, yellowish cloth, and where the skin showed, it was covered in long, grey hair.

Anderson reacted just in time, yanking Jensen away with a shout of shock and disgust. The door slammed shut, and they heard a low, creepy laugh from the other side.

Jensen hadn't seen anything, but when Anderson told him what had just happened, he became extremely shaken. He suggested they give up and lock themselves in one of their rooms.

Before they could act, the landlord returned with two strong men. All three looked nervous. Jensen rushed over and quickly explained everything that had happened. But his story only made the two men more scared—they dropped the crowbars they had brought and refused to go near the room.

The landlord was just as scared, torn between wanting to protect his hotel and not wanting to risk his life. Fortunately, Anderson found a way to motivate them.

"Is this the famous Danish bravery I've heard about?" he said. "It's not a German in there—and even if it was, we outnumber them five to one!"

The two workers and Jensen, embarrassed, pulled themselves together and rushed toward the door.

"Wait!" said Anderson. "Don't act without thinking. You—landlord—stay here with the light. One of you hit the door hard, but don't go inside right away if it opens."

The men nodded. The younger one stepped forward, raised his crowbar, and slammed it into the top panel of the door.

But what happened next shocked them all. The

wood didn't crack or break. Instead, the blow made a dull sound—like hitting a solid wall. The man dropped the crowbar with a cry and grabbed his sore elbow.

The noise made everyone turn to look at him, but when Anderson looked back at the door, it was gone. In its place was just a plain plaster wall with a large dent where the crowbar had hit. Room Number 13 had completely vanished.

For a few seconds, they all stood frozen, staring at the bare wall. In the silence, a rooster crowed from the yard below. Anderson turned toward the sound and saw through the window at the end of the hallway that the sky was beginning to lighten with the first signs of dawn.

***

"Maybe," the landlord said carefully, "you two might want to share a room tonight—one with two beds?"

Jensen and Anderson both agreed right away. After everything that had just happened, it felt much safer not to be alone. When they went to grab their things from their own rooms, they decided to go one at a time, with the other holding the candle and staying nearby. As they stepped into each room—Number 12 and Number 14—they both noticed something strange: each one had three windows.

***

The next morning, they all gathered again in Room 12. The landlord didn't want to call for outside help, but he knew they needed to solve the mystery in that part of the hotel. So, the two servants offered to help by doing the work themselves. They moved the furniture and, after breaking several wooden boards that couldn't be fixed, they pulled up the floor near Room 14.

You might expect they found a skeleton—maybe even Mag. Nicolas Francken's—but that wasn't what they uncovered. What they did find was a small copper box tucked between the beams under the floor. Inside was a carefully folded sheet of old parchment with about twenty lines of writing on it. Anderson and Jensen, who were both surprisingly good at reading old handwriting, got excited right away. They hoped the writing would finally reveal the truth behind all the strange things they'd experienced.

***

I own an astrology book that I've never actually read. At the front is a woodcut picture by Hans Sebald Beham showing several wise men sitting around a table. People who know about rare books might recognize it from that image. I don't remember the title, and I don't have it with me right now—but the inside covers are full of writing. In the ten years I've had it, I haven't been able to figure out which way the writing should be read, let alone what language it's in.

Anderson and Jensen were in a similar situation after they spent a long time studying the paper they found in the copper box.

After two days of staring at it, Jensen—who was a bit braver—guessed it might be written in Latin or Old Danish. Anderson didn't make any guesses and was happy to hand over the box and paper to the Historical Society of Viborg to keep in their museum.

A few months later, Anderson told me the whole story. We were sitting in the woods near Uppsala after visiting the library, where we'd looked at a strange old document. It was a contract where Daniel Salthenius— who later became a Hebrew professor in Königsberg— had sold his soul to the devil. I found it funny. Anderson didn't.

"What a fool," he said, meaning Salthenius, who was just a student when he did that. "Did he even know who he was getting involved with?"

When I offered the usual explanations, he just grunted. That same afternoon, he told me everything you've just read. But he wouldn't say what he thought it all meant—or even agree with the guesses I made.

The End

Thank You for Reading

Dear Reader,

We hope this timeless classic has sparked your imagination and enriched your literary journey. Now that you've turned the final page, we want to share a vision for the future of reading—one where every classic you've ever wanted to explore is at your fingertips, in a format that best suits your life.

We'd like to invite you to gain immediate, unlimited digital & audiobook access to hundreds of the most treasured literary classics ever written—along with the option to secure deluxe paperback, hardcover & box set editions at printing cost. Together, we can spark a new global literary renaissance alongside our small, independent publishing house called "The Library of Alexandria."

Thousands of years ago, the Library of Alexandria stood as a beacon of knowledge—until it was lost to history. We aim to reignite that spirit of preservation and discovery right now, in the modern age—only this time, it's accessible to all, in every language and every format.

Picture a world where every timeless classic, novel, poem, or philosophical treatise is not only available to read but also updated for today's readers—modernized, translated into any language or dialect, and ready to enjoy in any format you choose, whether that is in an eBook, audiobook, paperback, or deluxe hardcover & box set version a printing cost.

By joining our movement to rebuild the modern Library of Alexandria, you become part of an unprecedented mission to offer:

- **Unlimited Audiobook & eBook Access to the Greatest Classics of All Time**

  Instantly explore thousands of legendary works, from Plato and Shakespeare to Jane Austen and Leo Tolstoy. All are instantly ready to read or listen to, giving you a complete literary universe at your fingertips.

- **Paperback & Deluxe Editions at Printing Costs:**

  Purchase any title in a paperback, deluxe hardbound, or deluxe boxset edition at printing costs, shipped right to your doorstep. Curate your personal library of Alexandria with editions worthy of display— crafted to last, designed to captivate, and delivered straight to your door.

- **Modern translations for Contemporary Readers in all languages and dialects**

  Discover a vast selection of classics reimagined in clear, current language—no more struggling with outdated phrases or obscure references. Next to the original versions, we aim to offer translations in as many languages and dialects as possible.

  As we continue our translation efforts and add new languages, readers everywhere can connect with these works as if they were written today. By bridging linguistic divides, you're contributing to ensuring that these timeless stories become more meaningful, accessible, and inspiring for people across the globe.

- **Your Personal Library of Alexandria:**

  Over the months and years, you'll curate a unique physical archive of classics—each volume a testament to your taste, curiosity, and love of knowledge. It's not just about owning books—it's about curating a cultural legacy you'll cherish and pass down for generations to come.

- **Join a Global Literary Renaissance:**

  Your support fuels an ongoing mission: allowing us to reinvest in offering deluxe print editions (including special boxsets) at their true cost, broaden the range of available formats and translations, and extend the reach of these works to new audiences worldwide. By joining today, you're not just preserving a legacy of masterpieces; you set in motion a powerful wave of literary accessibility.

We are more than a publisher—we're a movement, and we can't do it alone. Your support lets us scale our mission, preserving and reimagining history's greatest works for tomorrow's readers.

Become a Torchbearer of knowledge.

Thank you for picking up this book and allowing us into your literary journey. As you turn the pages, know that you're part of something larger: a global effort to keep these stories alive, share their wisdom across borders and generations, and spark a true cultural revival for the modern era.

If this resonates with you—please consider taking the next step by visiting:

www.libraryofalexandria.com

With gratitude and a shared love of knowledge,

The Modern Library of Alexandria Team

Visit:

www.libraryofalexandria.com

Or scan the code below: